5 Minute Storytime

Children who are read to are inspired to read, so cuddle up for a 5 MINUTE STORYTIME and expand your child's mind as you build a lifelong love for reading and learning.

We cannot, however, guarantee your 5 minute break won't turn into 10, 15, or 30 minutes, as these FUN stories and engaging pictures will have you turning the pages AGAIN and AGAIN!

Designed by Flowerpot Press
in Franklin, TN.
www.FlowerpotPress.com
Designer: Stephanie Meyers
Editor: Katrine Crow
ROR-0811-0120
ISBN: 978-1-4867-1274-8
Made in China/Fabriqué en Chine

5 Minute Storytime

THE THREE BILLY GOATS GRUFF

RETOLD BY GEORGE BRIDGE

ILLUSTRATED BY IVANA FORGO

This is the story of three billy goats Gruff and a troll who did not know enough is enough. (Which may have been his undoing.)

This story happened some time ago, at a time when it was not that unusual for three billy goats to all have the same name.

Hi, Gruff!

Gruff was a quite popular name among billy goats back then and as it happened, these three friends were all named Gruff.

Hey, Gruff!

What's up, Gruff?

There was the SMALL billy goat Gruff, the BIG billy goat Gruff, and the BIGGEST billy goat Gruff.

There was also a troll, who shall remain nameless.

The troll lived under a bridge on a hillside where the three Gruffs liked to eat. One day, as they were wandering the hillside crunching on all the great green stuff they could see, they realized they had eaten most of what they could find on their side of the bridge.

So, one by one, the Gruffs decided to cross the bridge and head up the hill in search of more green snacks.

First came the SMALL billy goat Gruff to cross the bridge.
CLIP-CLOP, CLIP-CLOP went the billy goat's hooves on the bridge.

"What's that noise? Make it stop!" grumbled the troll.

"It's just me, the SMALL billy goat Gruff. I'm crossing your bridge to go look for a snack."

"Well, today you are going to be MY snack!" declared the troll.

"Oh no, don't eat me. I am much too little for a big troll like you. Another billy goat will be along shortly, and he is much BIGGER."

"Very well," said the troll. "Then be off with you. I want the BIG snack!"

And with that, the SMALL billy goat Gruff was free to go.

A short time later, the BIG billy goat Gruff came to the bridge.
CLIP-CLOP, CLIP-CLOP went the billy goat's hooves on the bridge.

"What's that noise? Make it stop!" grumbled the troll.

"It's just me, the BIG billy goat Gruff. I'm crossing your bridge to go look for a snack."

"Well, today you are going to be MY snack!" declared the troll.

"Oh no, don't eat me. A BIG troll like you should have the BIGGEST of snacks. Another billy goat will be along shortly and he is the BIGGEST."

"Very well," said the troll. "Then be off with you. I want the BIGGEST snack!"

And with that, the BIG billy goat Gruff was free to go.

Just a little while later, the BIGGEST billy goat Gruff came to the bridge. CLIP-CLOP, CLIP-CLOP went the billy goat's hooves on the bridge. It shook and creaked from the weight of the BIGGEST billy goat.

"What's that noise…" grumbled the troll nervously.

"It's just me, the BIGGEST billy goat Gruff. I'm crossing your bridge to go look for a snack."

"Well, today you are going to be MY snack..." the troll said meekly.

"Come on out from under that bridge and we will just see about that!" declared the BIGGEST billy goat Gruff.

"Very well," said the troll, nervously.

As the troll came out from under the bridge he saw the BIGGEST billy goat Gruff, and he knew right away he had made a mistake.

The **BIGGEST** billy goat Gruff used his two big horns to knock that troll back off the bridge and down the stream so far that he never returned.

And now all the billy goats and every other grazing animal on the hillside enjoy delicious snacks on both sides of the bridge without any trouble.

And that BIG bully of a troll was never ever seen again!

THE END.